AF355493

The
Very Special
Chromosome 21

ISBN: 978-93-55463-41-8
eISBN: 978-93-55463-42-5

© Publishers

Publisher: Pharos Books (P) Ltd.
Plot No.-55, Main Mother Dairy Road
Pandav Nagar, East Delhi-110092 (India)
Phone: +014049995474
WhatsApp: +014049995474
E-mail: sales@pharosbooks.in
Website: www.pharosbooks.in
Edition: 2022

THE VERY SPECIAL CHROMOSOME 21
Author: Epi Zeggou

Epi Zeggou

The
Very Special
Chromosome 21

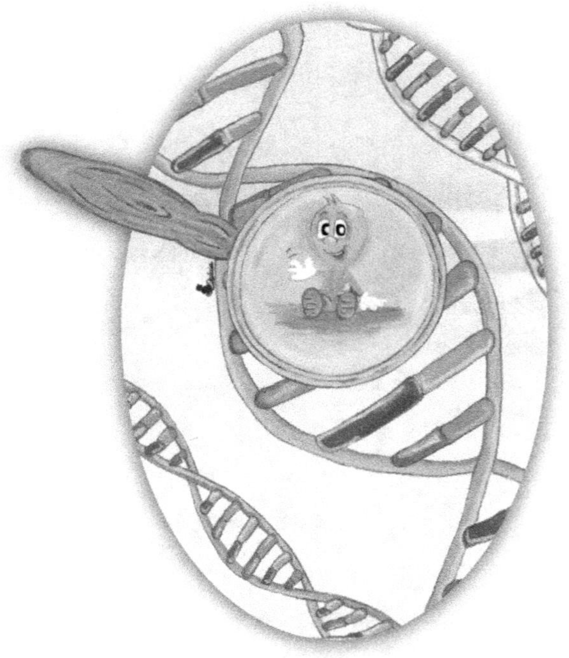

Illustrator: Theodosia Kotsika

Pharos Books

*…dedicated to John
to Nikola,
to Maria,
to Christina*

*and to all such special
and remarkable children,
born with Down syndrome
who came into the world to teach us
LOVE*

In memory of Paschalaki

Preface

When one meets families raising children with Down syndrome, one can only feel emotion and admiration. The calmness and sweetness that these people exude, despite their great anguish about the course and future of their children, in a society unprepared to accept and integrate them substantially, always impressed me.

 To these parents, as well as to every parent who experiences similar difficulties every day and has one more reason than the rest, to be anxious about the fate, health and future of their special child, we all owe a big thank you for the life lesson they offer us every day.

Epi Zeggou

A beautiful invitation with an all-white swan on a rich pink paper, tied with polychromous ribbons, arrived at the house. It was accompanied by a beautiful carousel bonbonière, full of colourful sugared almonds.

Myrto, who went to first grade and felt very proud to already know how to read, opened it and started reading in a loud voice.

"We invite you to our daughter's Christening on Sunday at the church of Panagitsa.

Your presence will give us great joy"

Parents - The Godmother

"Mum, Mum", she shouted cheerfully and ran towards her mother, waving the invitation and chewing as many sugared almonds as she could fit in her mouth, "on Sunday we have to go to a Christening" and quickly continued to speak without stopping. "Your friend Mrs. Hope baptizes her baby. We're going, aren't we? What am I going to wear? When are we going to get a gift for the baby?"

Her mother burst into laughter watching her excitement.

"Tomorrow afternoon, we're going to go shopping" she told her daughter.

From that moment Myrto counted the days left until Sunday, when she would go to the Christening. She had even prepared a drawing to give to the baby and secretly put it in the bag with the gift they had bought for her.

Finally, Sunday dawned.

Before her parents could wake up, Myrto had already got out of bed, washed her face, brushed her teeth and already worn her

prettiest dress.

She was very impatient.

She loved babies very much and as she had no siblings, she was very happy every time she was given the opportunity to meet a baby and play with other children.

All the way, she didn't stop singing, talking and laughing.

She was trying to imagine what the baby would look like, what name they would give her if she cried, and "could she hug the baby now that she's old enough and going to first grade?"

Arriving at the church her attention was drawn to the large balloons in pink and white colour forming a beautiful bouquet.

In the center, a large balloon in the shape of a heart had the name written up that the baby would take "DOROTHEA".

"That's a funny name, I've never heard of it" Myrto said, "what does it mean mum?"

"It means Gift of God, my little girl", her mother replied.

"Is that her grandmother's name?" she asked again.

"No, her parents chose it", her mother replied.

"And why didn't they choose another name? If they'd given her mine, I wouldn't mind". "This 'Dorothea' seems a little difficult and strange to me", Myrto commented.

"They chose this name, because the baby is for them a Gift from God", her mother replied.

"Well, you say the same thing about me and all parents about their children, but they don't call them all Dorothea, do they?"

"Why did they want to give her that particular name?" Myrto asked again.

"Because this baby is a special and remarkable child".

"Is that what you're saying? I don't understand what you mean when you say special".

"Shh!!!", the priest's voice was heard, "please be quiet, the Mystery starts".

Myrto left her mother's hand and headed with the other children to the baptismal font. She wanted so badly to see her new little friend up close.

Here she is, hugging her mother! Small blonde curls framed her face, two chubby hands hugged mum's shoulders. She wore a dress with painted butterflies and two very beautiful shoes with pink bows.

She was neither crying nor moaning, she was just sitting still and looking at her mother.

She didn't cry even when the priest plunged her into the baptismal font. Only when he lifted her up to put her in her godmother's arms, was she scared and began to cry loudly.

Myrto got closer, little Dorothea didn't look like the other babies she knew. Her blue eyes were a little slanted up, and from her half-open mouth, the tongue came out as if she were making fun of the world.

"I'll ask Mum later", she thought and along with the other children ran to taste the sweets and ice creams being shared for the Christening.

At the party followed, the little girl's parents danced excitedly, holding their daughter in their arms. All the guests ate, drank, danced, but they didn't laugh so much. It was a beautiful Christening, but Myrto felt a little strange.

The grandmother of the neophyte Dorothea, held

the little girl in her arms and talked to her, stroked her hair, sang to her, but... Myrto saw a tear slowly rolling down the cheek of the grandmother, which she hurriedly wiped with her hand before anyone else could realize it.

On the way back, Myrto had a bunch of questions, "Why was Dorothea like this? Why did she have her tongue sticking out all the time?" And "since she was tall why wasn't she walking yet, why wasn't she talking?"

"Why was her grandmother hugging her and crying? and why was everyone kind of... somehow... Myrto could not find the word... Well, they weren't as laughing and happy as at other Christenings she'd been to... and when she wished the parents for the little one why they were very serious?"

"Is she sick?"

"No, my little girl", her mother replied. "She's not sick, she's fine, she was just born a little different from the other kids, that's all".

"And how can anyone be born different?" Myrto asked full of curiosity.

"It can be done", her mother told her, it's a little hard to explain, but I'm going to try to tell you a story so you can understand it... And she started...

.... Once upon a time, not far away, there was a very strange country, **Cytoland**. Its houses were identical to each other and looked nothing like the houses we know. Each house was surrounded by a tall stone wall that inside, instead of a courtyard, there were a beautiful pond in which water lilies floated, small rock gardens with trees and flowers, artificial islets with playgrounds and golf courses. In the center of the pond there was a beautiful house and a very large and strange family lived in it. The **Chromosomuli** family.

Its members were so many that the dining table started from the kitchen, continued in the hallway and ended in the living room, so that all 46 Chromosomuli could fit in it!!!

Yes, that's right!! This family had 46 members. And they were all little kids. Very lively, skinny and cute little siblings who had the same strange name. They were called Chromosomes. And there was something even weirder. They were all twins. This strange family consisted of 23 twins!!!

First in line were the twin X Chromosome and Y Chromosome, followed by the twin Chromosome 1-A and Chromosome 1-B, Chromosome 2-A and Chromosome 2-B and thus continued until the last twins called Chromosome 22-A and Chromosome 22-B.

Of course because their names were, apart from strange and very large (can you imagine being called X Chromosome Chromosomulus or Chromosome 19-B Chromosomulus?) decided so as not to be confused to use only the number of their birth. So, all day at home, you could hear them shouting some strange numbers and letters together that you were confused about, and you didn't know if you were in a house where kids live or in a robot factory.

"3-A put down myyyyyyy pencils!!!"

"9-B eats my food!!!"

"Yuck! 22-B has snots and cries!!"

"Pooh!!! 22-A again pooped and stinks!!"

They were having a wonderful time with play and laughter and in the evenings all the siblings gathered around the fireplace, told fairy tales and before they went to bed they hugged each other and promised that they would always be so united and loved!!!

The years passed, the children grew up and no longer fit in their beautiful little house.

So one day, when they were all gathered, the older siblings, X and Y, announced to them that the time had come to separate.

You can't describe what happened. They all started crying together, shouting, screaming and saying: "This is never going to happen, and that they would all stay together. Isn't that what they said every night? Now, what's changed?"

The older siblings, very calmly explained to them that like them, there are in Cytoland countless families of Chromosomuli who when just grow up enough, the twins are divided into two equal groups.

One team takes one sibling and the other one its twin.

Each group consists of 23 Chromosomuli who live together in the same house, but separate from the rest of their siblings.

"That's why all Chromosomuli are made", they explained.

"In the new house we're going to go to, we'll move in with 23 other Chromosomuli

from another family and together we're going to work together and make something wonderful. A miracle that only we can do. A new life!"

They had no choice so the siblings embraced, kissed, promised that they would never forget each other and set off for their new home. But then something strange happened.

The smallest kids who had the number 21 decided they didn't want to split up.

So one of them hid well and went with its twin sibling.

At first, the rest of its siblings were very happy to see it, but when they met the other 23 roommates, the problems began.

That's because in the new house there was only room for **46** people and they were now **47**.

So they had a hard time cooking, eating, sleeping, playing. Everything was happening at a slower pace.

And when the time came for everyone to work together to create 'the miracle' there, things got more difficult. The little 21 that was there, would go around and mix everything up. There was no work for the naughty 21, and yet it wanted to do something so badly!!!

When their older siblings and the other 23 new roommates worked to-gether, the little and naughty 21 went and cheated, changed their plans and made

corrections to make itself feel like it had a role, too.

And it's true that it did too much damage.

It changed everything, nothing happened as originally planned. The cunning little 21 left its mark everywhere.

At first, the others got angry but they decided to help the 21 and try together for the 'miracle'.

And at some point they made it.

The miracle happened.
A new life has been created.
A baby!!!

The newborn was, of course, a little different from the others, but this baby was created by the love of their parents and had come into the world to live and be happy.

There was a baby who stood out from the rest because the child had something the other babies didn't have. An extra chromosome. The very naughty, lively and playful 21, who didn't want to part from its twin.

The baby's parents, when they first saw their child, felt embarrassed, froze, never imagined that the first moment they would hold their child in their arms would be such.

Then, they got worried, sad, angry with themselves, mad at the doctors who didn't inform them that their baby would be born so different, angry even with God who surprised them by giving them a child that didn't look like the others. "How would they be able to raise this child properly?" they wondered.

They'd heard that sometimes from a game of chromosomes, some children didn't look like the rest, they even had some distant acquaintances who, with a lot of love, with almost adoration, raised such a special child.

But because they didn't know much about these children, they were afraid.

And fear of the unknown brings anger and sadness.

And when they were thinking about whether they'd make it, something unexpected happened. The baby slowly turned the head, opened their little slanted up eyes and looked towards their mother. That's it!!! At once, all the worries and doubts disappeared.

The innocent gaze of the little angel gave the solution to their questions. It was their baby, their own special baby who would grow up in as much care and love as they could give.

Because love is the one that manages and defeats all obstacles and difficulties and fills every family with joy and happiness.

The days, the months passed, the baby was growing. The parents loved that little creature who was the whole world to them. It is true that many times it was very difficult, there were moments when they felt frustrated and helpless, but one smile was enough to give them strength and hope.

The baby was growing at their own slower pace.

The infant did all the things a baby does, cried when they were hungry, moaned when they were sleepy and wanted a hug, but, having trouble catching their toys, they couldn't stand up in their playpen and preferred to sit on their cot while spending endless hours, smiling happily in their mother's arms.

And their parents were always close to them and talked to them, sang to them, read them fairy tales, tried to help them do all the things that another baby at this age would do, but that their little one needed a lot of effort to make it...

The truth is, those early years were very, very difficult. Their baby differed quite a bit from other children their age in both appearance and behaviour, and this often made them uncomfortable. They felt the eyes of passers-by in the street full of curiosity, unwittingly listening to the naive questions and innocent comments of the children about the child's appearance every time they took their kid for a walk in the stroller.

How much they would like to shout to the whole world that this little child, this little treasure sent to them by God had the same rights in life as the other children who were all proud to walk in the square and bragged about their first words and steps. How much they would want to tell all these people that their little angel had been fighting since the first moment they were born and would fight all their life to achieve the simplest things, the first words, the first steps and how proud they felt every time their child managed to do something.

They would love to share the joy and pride they felt when, two years since the day this special child came into the world, opened his chubby hands and said like all the children of the world ... Mum!!!

They would so much like to brag about their child's exploits like all parents, but they feared that people wouldn't understand them, they couldn't be happy with them because they had learned to deal reluctantly and awkwardly with everything different.

Time was passing. The kid was growing up. Slowly, the child started with the help of the parents, the special therapists and teachers and after a lot of effort to walk, talk, play with their toys.

The child loved listening to music and waving their feet to its beat.

So happy was the kid every time they played ball with their father and laughed happily when they went with him to the playground.

They enjoyed hitting the pots with two wooden spoons and stirring up the house with their fuss and voices.

The child played, like all kids play, they said little words, laughed when they were happy, cried very loudly and cried when they were sad, they did everything a little kid does, they just did it in their own special and different way, slower and noisier.

And so the years passed, the child grew old enough and it was time to go to school.

His parents were struggling. How would the other children react with a child other than them in their class?

Who would be able to explain to the other children that this special and different child needed a lot of tenderness and calm? That this kid needed more time, more effort and enough help to understand and do all the things their classmates easily did on their own.

That this child could not do so well in the lessons, that they could have difficulty speaking clearly, writing and reading, but they had no difficulty laughing with their heart and opening their hands embracing all the people in their big arms?

Were the other children ready to take such a special creature into their company?

They knew that many times young children can become very hard and hurt with the words or actions their classmates. They knew that people often become unfair and mean to people who are a little different from others. They didn't want that to happen, they never wanted anyone to upset their little angel because that kid was a little angel. This child had a pure, clean look, a child without malice, without cunning who spoke only the language of truth, did not understand lies and hypocrisy and knew how to love the whole world with all the power of their soul.

Even when they were angry, scared, sad, even when their loud voices and tears stirred the world, that was because they felt very, very bad and showed it in any way they could.

And that made them so special. Their sincerity and innocence.

This child was a special one, a Gift from God, who came to life to teach everyone that the most important thing in the world is LOVE.

A tender little creature who appeared as a playful surprise in their parents' life and upset it, while at the same time giving them the privilege of raising a little angel in their family. An angel whose smile warmed everyone's hearts. That's why this angel was most dear.

At school, everyone was close to them to help them, everyone wanted this kid to be in their company, because the child's innocent smile and good heart overflowing with tenderness and love were precious to all.

This little one was so special because this child knew how to love and was very happy to have conquered from the first moment what all people struggle to

win.

ACCEPTANCE AND LOVE!!!

Mum turned around and looked at Myrto. She was smiling half-asleep in the back seat of the car.

"Mum, you know what? It was very nice meeting Dorothea and I think we will be good friends. I'm so glad to have such a special friend in my life", she said and fell asleep happily.

The End

Let's *play* **now.**

Come on, let's play the quiz game.
Let's see how many correct answers you'll give:

1. What gift did Myrto prepare for the little baby?
A packet with colourful sugared almonds.
A carousel game.
A drawing.

2. What name was written on the big balloon?
Theodora
Hope
Myrto
Dorothea

3. What did Myrto notice when she saw the baby for the first time?
That the baby was too big.
That the baby was kind of different and very special.
That the baby wasn't walking.

4. Why was the baby so different and special?
Because the baby was sitting quietly in their mother's arms and didn't cry.
Because the baby had a little slanted up eyes.
Because the baby had an extra chromosome 21.

5. When the baby got a little older, what did the infant like to do?
Listening to music and waving their feet to its beat.

Going to the playground and playing ball with dad.
Making mischief.

6. *The child grew up and it was time to go to school.
Why do you think the other kids wanted the kid in their
company?*
Because the kid was playing ball.
Because the kid gave them sweets and ice-creams
during breaks.
Because the kid had an innocent smile and a big
tender heart full of love for all.

And now let's talk.

How did this extra chromosome get into the baby?
To create a new life, chromosomes from two different families need to work together. Each time 23 chromosomes from one family and 23 chromosomes from the other family work together.

Sometimes, however, in some family there can be a very lively, cunning and naughty chromosome (the little 21) that does not want to separate from its twin and so always goes with it. The baby born then, will have one more chromosome and more specifically, will have an extra chromosome 21. Babies therefore have trisomy 21 (i.e. three chromosomes 21) or Down syndrome.

And how is it possible for a single extra chromosome to cause so many changes for the baby to be born?
When time comes for the 23 chromosomes of one family to work together with the 23 chromosomes of the other family, the little 21 that is left over, goes and gets involved in the work of the other chromosomes. It confuses them and makes mistakes, distracts them with its mischief and makes its own plans. As a result, too many changes are being made.

What changes can the small and colourful chromosome 21 make?
It can do a lot of things. Some of them are visible, for example: this is what changes the shape of the eyes

and is somewhat slanted up, this is what draws the tongue to grow a little more so that many times (not always) it sticks out of the baby's mouth.

Some changes though it makes are not immediately visible, but we understand them when we see a child with an extra chromosome 21 playing, talking, reading, moving. Everything is done at a slower and different pace. And that's because the very naughty EXTRA chromosome 21 confuses its siblings, so they can't coordinate easily as a team. So children born with an extra chromosome 21 need more time and much more effort to achieve something.

Does this chromosome do only cheats?
No, of course not, it does a lot of beautiful things.

It makes the hearts of these young children so big and clean that they fit and love the whole world. It teaches this kid never to lie, to always tell the truth, to smile a lot and love and help their friends. These aren't few. In fact, they are the most important things one can learn.

If I meet such a special child, how am I supposed to treat them?
Normally, as you treat all your friends and classmates. The fact that this kid has an extra chromosome in their body than you and the rest of your friends shouldn't affect your behaviour.

You all have the same need for love, friendship, affection

and companionship. You all want to play, get to know the world, learn new things, have fun. It's just that your new friend will express their wishes a little differently. Your friend will need more time to make it, more attention and care from parents and teachers and they will want their friends to be more patient with them.

That's all.

Nothing else.

I'd like to know more about these special kids.

All the children in the world are different from each other. Each is born with a different combination of the genetic code (the order in which chromosomes stand opposite each other so as to be able to work together) of their parents. This combination determines their potential (what they could be done) at a rate of 50%. But their evolution (i.e., what they will be) is determined by the other 50% of their environment, namely their family, friends, teachers, the school environment, the country they grow up in, the places they visit, the stimuli they get, the fairy tales and books they read, the studies they will do, how much they will play and exercise out in nature with their friends, how healthily they will eat, whether they listen or learn to play music, if they learn to dance, make crafts and many more.

Children born with an extra chromosome also respond, others to a greater extent and others to a lesser extent to the stimuli they receive from their environment, like all children in the world. They fight, they learn, they choose their friends, they adapt, they love. They can attend classes, learn to play music, write, read, cook, dance, make wonderful crafts, work when they grow up and become best friends.

It all depends to a large extent on the people who will be close to them and support them, as is the case with all the children in the world. Pablo Pineda, Maria Nitsa, Annarose Rubright, Rachel Handlin, Zohar Silok, Hannah Sampson, Ellie Goldstein, Yulissa Arescurenaga, Debora de Moura, Chelsea Werner , Collette Divitto, Loxandra Lucas, Lauren Potter, James Brewer, Tommy Jessop, Chris Burke, Edward Barbanell, Mr. Stevens, Eleni Louka ,Ioakim Frossinis, are just some of the people who have managed to stand out and stand out around the world. Down syndrome didn't stop them from making their dreams come true and becoming happy.

Did you know that?

March 21st is a day dedicated to children with this extra chromosome.

The World Day for Down Syndrome was established in 2006 with the encouragement of the Greek geneticist and Professor of Genetics at the Medical School of the University of Geneva, Mr. Stylianos Antonarakis, who is the scientist that mapped the sequence of chromosome 21, namely in very simple words, he recorded the route they follow and the ways in which chromosomes work each time to create these so special and remarkable children with the extra chromosome 21. In fact, in an interview, the professor explained why he proposed this date, "I chose March 21st not by accident, since it is the third month of the year and people with Down have three chromosomes 21 instead of two".

40

Epi Zeggou was born in 1969 in Larissa, Greece. Mother of three, she is an Msc DVM. She entered the world of writing with her essay "Journey into the World of Dementia" written in her father's memory as an effort to help inform people and support families experiencing the problem of Dementia.

On the occasion of this essay, she presented a paper in the 9th Panhellenic Congress of Alzheimer's Disease and Related Disorders (Thessaloniki, May 2015) entitled Dementia as Seen through the Perspective of the Caregiver. The rights of the essay have been conceded by the author to the Greek Association of Alzheimer's Disease and Related Disorders "Alzheimer Hellas". She has also established an online support team for patients with Dementia.

In 2015 she launched the fairytale "The Very Special Chromosome 21", also granting the rights of the Greek version, to the Association of Parents and Friends of People with Down Syndrome of Thessaly "The Swan". Without ever having the experience of Down Syndrome in her close family and relatives, The Very Special Chromosome 21, is her effort to raise awareness and promote understanding for a sensitive and serious social issue as the Down Syndrome

The fairytale "My Grandpa and Mr. Alzheimer" is her third book which was also presented as a paper in the 11th Panhellenic Congress of Alzheimer's Disease and Related Disorders entitled "The Fairytale as a Mental Tool".

In the recent 12th Panhellenic Congress of Alzheimer's Disease, she was the President of the round table with the distinguished lecture "The role of the media in the awareness of Alzheimer Disease".

And... let's meet our illustrator

Theodosia Kotsika was born in 1983 in Galatini village in the municipality of Kozani, Greece. She holds a degree in Agriculture Engineering. She studied seven years at the Community Cultural Centre at the Painting Department in Kozani. Painting is her greatest love. She illustrated "The Very Special Chromosome 21" followed by "My Grandpa and Mr Alzheimer" by Epi Michi-Zeggou. She uses diverse materials making her works vivid and unique. She has created wonderful murals, photo wallpapers and outstanding paintings. She also draws on fabrics and clothes. Her work is characterized by its strong realism with an emphasis on detail while combining elements of fantasy and imagination. Go to her Facebook account sleepycat. art and immerse into the magic of her works.

Michaella L. Gerogioka-Tsoutsouka was born in 1972 in Larissa, Greece. She holds a MA in Translation and Interpreting by the University of Sheffield, an MA in Education by The Open University, a BA in English and Linguistics and a Diploma in English Literature by the University of Westminster. She is the Director of her English Center in Larissa where not only does she teach English to Greek students but also collaborates with numerous EU institutions, UNESCO, multi-national companies, municipalities and universities providing translation and interpretation services. She is married to Nick Tsoutsoukas, mother of two and loves painting, travelling and reading.

www.ingramcontent.com/pod-product-compliance
Lightning Source LLC
LaVergne TN
LVHW051241200726
843510LV00011B/1638